THE WORDS I KNOW

The Words I Know

CATHY STONEHOUSE

PRESS GANG PUBLISHERS
VANCOUVER

Some of the poems in this book have been published previously in *The Malahat
Review, Prairie Fire, grain, CV2, Tessera, Fireweed, Room of One's Own, Canadian Woman
Studies* and *The Capilano Review*.

The epigraph by Frida Kahlo is excerpted from *Frida, a biography of Frida Kahlo*,
by Hayden Herrera (New York: Harper & Row, 1983), p. 75.
The excerpt by Di Brandt, on p. 74, is from *mother, not mother* (Stratford, Ont.: The
Mercury Press, 1992), pp. 54–55.

The publisher gratefully acknowledges financial assistance from the Canada Council
and the Cultural Services Branch, Province of British Columbia.

Canadian Cataloguing in Publication Data

Stonehouse, Cathy.
The words I know

   Poems.
   ISBN 0-88974-037-2

   I. Title.
PS8587.T66W67 1994   C811'.54   C94-910671-2
PR9199.3.S76W67 1994

Editor for the Press: Barbara Kuhne
Cover and chapter opening illustrations are from an original
   collage, *Marsden Rock*, by Ian Stonehouse, © 1994
Design and typesetting: Val Speidel
Typeset in Perpetua
Printed on acid-free paper
Printed and bound in Canada by Best Book Manufacturers Inc.

Press Gang Publishers
101-225 East 17TH Avenue
Vancouver, B.C. V5V 1A6
Canada

for Ian

A little while ago . . . I was a child who went about in a world of colors, of hard and tangible forms. Everything was mysterious and something was hidden, guessing what it was was a game for me. If you knew how terrible it is to know suddenly, as if a bolt of lightning elucidated the earth. Now I live in a painful planet, transparent as ice.

FRIDA KAHLO, 1926

Acknowledgements

I would like to thank the Canadian Commonwealth Scholarship Commission for granting me the two-year scholarship to the University of British Columbia that supported my M.F.A. studies, during which time this book was begun.

I would also like to thank the following people who have given invaluable support and advice during the writing and editing of these poems: Daphne Marlatt, Keith Maillard, George McWhirter, Barbara Parkin, Mary Cameron, Mark Cochrane, Melissa Jacques and Wayne Hughes. Thanks to Suniti Namjoshi for her wise and insightful comments and for encouraging me to publish, and to all the women from West Word 1993 for helping me find my voice.

Thanks to Barbara Kuhne, Val Speidel and Della McCreary for all their creative and respectful work, and for giving me this opportunity to realize a dream.

Thanks to Misri Dé for bringing Frida to my attention at a crucial moment (and for looking so much like her); to Alexa Berton for sensitive photography; to my mother for passing on to her children a creative warrior spirit; to my brother Ian for the cover artwork, for being my collaborator in creativity and survival all these years, and for inventing cheese sunglasses; to Wayne for everything, especially constancy.

Special thanks to all the friends, helpers, fellow writers and survivors past and present whose names are not mentioned here—for all your support, inspiration and nurturing both individually and cumulatively; thanks to my two cats, especially Nimbus, whose trips across the keyboard always open me to new possibilities; thanks to the rain.

Contents

THE ENORMOUS EXIT

ASK YOUR FATHER

Drought summer

Our butterfly bush grew out from the fence
like never before. Each blossom swelled
and the fat sun caught like buttered crumbs
between the tangling fronds. All day
I watched it from the garden path, watched
the ring-marked wings of the red admiral
open like darkened pores on every stem—

we put the moth trap out at dusk.
I counted the first ten moths
that flew into the bare white bulb,
heard their wings rattle
at the metal rim, saw them fold
like flattened paper cups, then went inside.

My brother used the bathroom first.
After he'd finished I would lock the door,
switch the light on, and unpeel
the sticky layers of my summer clothes,
lifting one arm to count
each tiny hair that blossomed in the dip beneath.

Later, I'd feel the thickening tips
of where my breasts would be—
nipples that rasped all day against my shirt
crumpled beneath the night's dry surfaces,
two soft wingbuds, pointed as if for flight.

Ask your father

"I was never artistic,"
says my grandmother,
slicing a hard-boiled egg
into delicate rounds,
wiping wet shell pieces
onto her homemade apron,
"but our Peter's been good with his hands."

"I'm no bright spark,"
says my aunt,
unpacking the foil dinosaur
she made at the hospital school,
"it's only eggboxes.
Your uncle has all the ideas."

"I can't think straight,"
says my mother, pressing pleats
into my brother's jeans,
one eye on the clock
while the oven heats up,
her library book propped by the sink.
"Your father's the one with the brains."

We just went for a walk, mum

we just went for a walk down the Dane it was cold we were
hobbits we had sticks cow parsley with the end knocked off ian
jumped in a cowpat we played poohsticks mine got caught on a
rock not fair on the bridge we watched how the river ran dirty
smelly over the field past the new power station and the old
farmer's bulls i was scared but the long grass hid my red wellies
phew we were on a Journey i had a Horse it was called Stallion
ian's was called Red Ned suddenly there were bricks we were at
the viaduct big navvies built it ian said there were bricks fallen
everywhere he made me stand underneath i was scared then the
train came rumbling overhead i screamed it echoed ian waved at
the train it was going to crewe he knew its name i screamed i
sang oh come all ye faithful it was ace brilliant it was like chester
cathedral it was like a big fridge a rumbling fridge all cold and
echoey then we came home there was a white horse it ran it
chased us i lost the toggle-thing off my coat horsey waited at the
gate we ran up the hill we were hobbits except with wings i flew
over the stile we were on the road it was london road there were
cars one like mr jeff's we laughed we started to run we laughed
we blew underarm farts and picked off dandelion heads all the
way back down the hill

Consequences

Cowpats fry in flies,
in every handful of grass
we find sharpened blades and the river's
feverish, barely moving.
This bough at the bend holds me
where kingfishers skim the brown skin
of the river then fly on;
even here, the current twists
and rolls towards lower ground.

Why did we look into that doorway?
Our parents
naked as fluttering moths across the bed
I only saw a crack and then ran.
On a distant road real cars
compress heat into melting tarmac,
on the railway bridge travellers
in second-class compartments
drum their fingers along dusty seats;
every sound has its reason.
The closed-up air of our house
drifting secretly into the street,
his white hands holding her down.
We could play man and wife but we know too much.
I pick at berries while you
whittle sticks, all distance between us
measured out in telegraph poles,
the tall giant-strides of the fields.

What if he, what if she—
the view I have yields broken sentences,
the livid green hum of the trees
their June-hot exhalations
already blurs what I came here for,
running through the grass, following you
for a reason.

Rubbed out

Night comes in
and changes the shape of our street.
Deck chairs folded and put away,
streetlight catches the vinyl hair
of dolls abandoned amongst dry grasses,

each house now moored like a boat
by a slim rope of path
to the floating dark, all space between
rippling, widened.

Adult feet erase chalk marks,
blunt arrows and hopscotch squares
pointed at the setting sun;

lit buildings
are veiled by curtains and blinds.
The sounds outside
elongate
like rails along a rickety bridge
struggling to connect—
door slam, feet shuffled home
from pub or late shift,
the hum of traffic, or stars.

My brother is watching the stars

My brother is watching the stars tonight
from a folding chair on the lawn,
my father's sheepskin coat draped round
his narrow shoulders, touching his boots,
and the wooden legs of the chair indent the turf.
His nails are bitten down to half moons,
his grip on my father's binoculars turns
his knuckles white, he gazes south
into the night sky, and waits
for the reddish light of Mars to prick each lens.

My father is watching my brother tonight
from the garden path, without his coat,
he is watching my brother's hands,
he is standing silent, arm folded to chest,
his last cigarette still lit when it reaches the grass.
Blood vessels burn red spots into his cheeks,
his shirt hangs out over a belt
round his shrunken waist, his lungs
whistle unevenly as he focusses on
the small white galaxy of breath round my brother's mouth.

I am watching my father and brother tonight
from the upstairs room, my torch is off.
The stars sprawl wide above the trees,
I do not know their names. I watch
the tilt of my father's face, my brother's back:
they float like astronauts through
the uneven darkness, and I see
no light, no silver cord that holds them
there; my chest feels tight and small.
My brother waits for Mars; my father waits.

Thirteen

The curtains half open,
maybe someone from the street
can see in.
The chant of cars
homecoming across a quiet bridge
repeats itself,
a gentle rim of sound.

Inside my room
white flowers in a jar
bend forwards
with their lips open, silent—

silent too in the mirror's world
where cupped hands form
a line through which my body falls,
falling into line.

Glistening palettes spread across my desk
show all the colours I could paint myself.
As night's sharp leaves
proliferate beneath my skin,
through the looking glass
my mouth surfaces
like grief
in another language:

something is missing.

The snowman

He had the coldest of hands.
I look down a shrinking tunnel
at the dazzling sight of him, breath smoke
livid as he patiently moves
the sticks of my small body around.
I did not expect him to wake like this.
He has taken out the coals of his eyes
ripped out his carrot stick nose
removed the red scarf that separated head from neck
and become all snow: his voice, his teeth
still glittering.
Ticklish at first, then anxious,
hoary fingers holding me down as he peels off
my cold weather clothes.
It's as if he's trying to press me
to his own fat shape. As he enters

there's a ripping
and I try to remember the field's surface
compacted by my own hands into ice,
each rolled ball collected in a long bandage:
now his face breaks off in pieces,
clearer and clearer becoming not my own.
The world pressed flat
into a framed picture,
my limbs elongate, distant and overexposed.

When I reach for my lips
I cannot find them —
I need to find some stones
for eyes, a row of small pebbles
for my mouth: I know I'll have to lie,
later on.

Soil

Angered, your glasses fly
in slow motion towards the wall
lenses shattered into senseless jewels
you are turning towards me
hands mouth eyes
striking the same tuneless note

I am dirty, I know I am
skin quivering, lungs
contracted to the size of buttons
voiceless, staring
behind you to the chair

you told me earlier how
rabbits breed, why
songbirds die and that
there's nothing nice to look at
when you're dead but darkness, darkness and soil

Crossing the road

Only once
I looked you in the eye,
when something tugged you
from the inside
and we both saw the suture twitch.

I am Jim, you said,
here is my signature,
written with one hand
wiped out with the other.

Alone on the back doorstep,
eyes turned into the blind alley,
thumb and finger rolling
at an absent speck,

I know you are my father.
You do the things that fathers
always do, slam glass doors
until the dense pane cracks,
fondle me with unseeing eyes.

Your rough hands
cradle each cigarette
against an adult wind,

red mouths smouldering
on concrete, I know I must
stamp on their burning ends.

When your body begins dying,
ligaments in a middle finger
shorten, close your hand
into a loose, permanent fist.

With scarcely any breath
you phone to ask me for
another pack of fags,
Mackeson's stout for your liver,
no cure left for your heart.

Breath

As he died, my father's heart
fell in on itself
like a worked-out mineshaft
and the sound in his chest
was of an underground stream.
He could not draw breath to say
how the water filled his lungs
how his chest wall fluttered
like the ground during a subsidence
when the pitwheel has stopped turning
and there's nothing left to do but watch;

he had no breath to whisper
that what lived in him then
was his home, Whitburn Colliery
one hundred back-to-back houses
two chapels and a school
how they levelled it out
grassed it over
when the coal stopped surfacing.

What died with him
when his tongue arched back
were the lives of the men
who sat on the beach, unmoving
like tools abandoned before the coalface
hands empty in their pockets
silent, because they had no breath left
to cry out with, nothing to do but watch
how the turf grew thick above the mineshaft,
even the gulls flew south, and the wind
blew straight above their heads, in from the sea.

Stolen

With a ball high on wind
slapping into my hand
I pretend I can feel nothing:
thick as turf laid deep over bricks
dead colliers lived between,
wind pinching my throat
making your car keys spin on their plastic chain

You catch my ball, and I crouch
speechless in squeaking grass
rake my pockets privately
for something beautiful to sell
to get me out of here—

Marsden Green, false carpet
rolled over colliery slag
studded with fretwork benches
peeled paintskin hangs off in folds—

Marsden Rock, arched
in a bow that will never break
sodden with birdshit, pebbles and sand—

shell-studded Grotto,
where you scald your hands
on a pot of fresh tea
and I melt into your soft cruel face,
the birds loose as tickets,
the steep foothills of the waves

where an upturned hulk rolls its rusty eyeball:
caught on a reef since you were a boy
nothing shifts it, though trawlers
have long since taken away the crew

have long since stolen
my imaginary drowning sailors,
trapped between salt-licked whips of sea
and the stones' sharpness,
who are counting the brown-knuckled hands of the waves
that open like yours to fill every crevice
and never never give up.

Dear god——

Not enough blue sky
to make a cat a pair of trousers.

By my feet, waves unwind
a white spool, brief mess of thread.

The fluid atlantic, sober grey
and without mind, carries his great welsh grief
from one long shore to the next. Prayerful

I photograph the wind, whipcrack in the sky
that separates two worlds,

harsh anatomy of your absence;

sea lettuce, sea stars
perfect as children's splayed hands.

Illuminations

From a different coast you come to me
up the dark stairs, lights have been turned off
your flattened feet are bare, the weapon
hangs half-stiff between cotton flaps
secure in its power to induce the drowning element.
Be a good quiet girl. Be a good still dead quiet girl.
You climb up the slope of the seaside town
where you learned this trade,
past rocks where the lighthouse flickers,
mounting the steps to your own full size, the sheen
on your quiet flesh exuding its own numinous light.
This is for you, and you and you and you, Mummy.
It's in between her fine striations that you'll bury me,
beyond the calculation of the beams, in the cove by the beach
where you buried memory.
As you open the bedroom door
you embrace the family seal,
its convex injunctions
emboss
into soft red wax
what you learned of the symbols 'father', 'daughter'.

I am six years old, afraid to move my eyes
in this body that the dark has given me,
pin-pricked by thin subtle sounds.
I'm waiting
on a cliffhead in my long white gown
for your rippling movements
there undressing beside the bed,
I know that I am doomed to die at sea
your cold white body rising
from the water, solid and vast
against which my tiny mind founders,
a neat wooden vessel, a tinkling Marie Celeste.

Dark hair fanning out, green hands clutching at my neck
I'd swallow but there's no room:
I've seen far down your throat
to where the tongue lies down and cannot speak.
I'm soft and toothless in my shell
black roots of hairs stand out on your upper lip
lie still Cathy lie still
and what of the words I know?

Night-time   seabird   father
pubic bone slams against chest
if we are both vessels mine is full yours empty
when our masts clink together mine has a tinny sound.

II.

hate no i love you no i
love no i hate you

carved into a grand figurehead, my
head and lungs
turned to wood

daddy

light
strikes your body
like a thin crown, cracks open eyes
like a whip, i can see

everything see
everything i needed to know
needed to know to live
inside you, hush

is this anchor hooked
around which i turn

III.

The wind is up
the night's a buttonhook
pulls me
out of all this
tangling, pulled
through the eye of ceiling
that closes to seal you in

nothing moves below
the street lies flat as an ache

while your hair fills my mouth
I rise above our house
lost in the logic of other houses
the map of the ever-repeating
night, imagine

unclothed on the bed
bound wings chafing at my chest
how I travel

flying low above the river ridges
past the motorway
the tramp with his seven coats
snoring in a rusty van
on the road to Scotland

travel past all thoughts of tomorrow
to where tarmac meets the sea:
Blackpool, dreaming of the night
they turn the lights on

you can make me dance
but up here strings of light unfurl
miraculous, gaudy
from my mouth

I burp forth elephants
china dogs, whirlwinds
watch the big wheel dip
and the tower door fly open

where an old man plays an organ
made of tiny children's toes

A child's garden (of verses)

Little stunted rhymes in pots
on the window ledge
trying to put forth blooms
while outside it rains and
inside grandma combs tats from my hair
saying sit still what's wrong
with this child? and i

make up sayings like "purple
flowers thunder showers"
"once upon a time there was
a squashed fly stuck in a
bowl of porridge who"
etc. waiting
until she's finished
the rain's finished they're all
finished i can put a big
full stop at the end of every

sentence listen to the
music of the grass
telling me without words
who to be.

PHANTOM PAIN

Anniversary

The white skin
that heals between two days
is the slice that terror has taken.

November, metallic equinox.

The creak of an iron hinge,
the clink of spoon
laid down on a polished hospital tray,
your watch strap unbuckling:

caught in its leghold trap
I peel back memory,
its glinting seam
unzipping all the riches of the earth.

As the metal jaws of death
closed upon you, something in me
was released: a hare

across the hard blue openness
your hands leaving me
had left; laid out
for the first time
across the map of coming winter,
your crystalline trapper's bones.

Phantom pain

I hear it all still: sheep's bleat on the moor
and the peewee's thin call in the weeds.

KEN SMITH, The Poet Reclining

Sharp click of latch
into the garden shed.
Cigarette butts
mangled in the ashtray
a dry unfinished paragraph.

I touch cheap crystal, my hand
stunned as a bird on window glass
to recollect

the stone of his cold body,
clogged lungs cradled by a skin
bright and smooth as if
polished.

Daylight stripes
the tall wooden limb
of a spade, empty glove
my hand warms to, nerves colliding
with the reach of his dead fist.

I can hear the bright scratch
of sulphur on wood, the hiss
of his breath, catching:

never forgive.

Magic lantern

We are children stumbling through fog:

my father's breath, white
and silent, blurs
into my baby arms
placed around his neck like a fur.

I overturn chairs
in our back garden,
you play a small guitar too fast
bow to the camera
and we are specks of dust
an amber glow fading to grainy black.

Do I call this memory?

The light in the film unbandaging
thick and luminous as kitchen curtains
all it does not show:

The year you crushed your Airfix models underfoot
plastic spitfires cracking into dust,

when they tested the three-minute siren
on the roof of our school
and we did nothing but listen, carry on
our lives blown thin across the chem lab walls
bunsen-blue, brief experiments.

Swallow down the nineteen seventies
store them in labelled boxes,

unreeled into
this unstable element
you hold up to the light:

the magic lantern

full of shadow-horses, full of children

who run and run
strain their necks but never quite
break the tape.

Rapes revisited

Now I hold you in my arms
hot from the bunched-up blankets
burning rasp of flesh and hairs

small hands gloved inside mine
shrinking towards memory
the sound of radios, the man
who is in the room is in the room
is in me, breath sharp
eyes rolled back as if in death

look away oh look away from
the deep hole he puts you in
the thing itself you resist
with all the space you have

hands grasp legs jerk
sound flies out
hits the wall and does not break—

BANDAGES

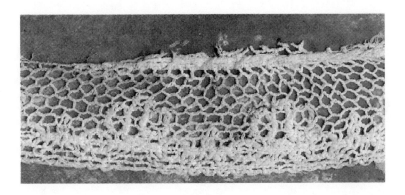

At the border

When I arrive,
dead heads of roses
will be scattered on the kitchen floor.
Tonight you sing to me,
my hat pulled low above your eyes,
while distant villages dazzle us like fairgrounds,
their orange lights revolving as we swing
towards the unlit north.

In Catalonia, the body of christ
still trembles on its handmade cross,
driving and driving blood's heat through barren fields.
As our train pulls out from Lérida
the scent of rosemary
drifts in from half-lit hills;

easter mountains settle dark as smoke
into the tracks behind. Women
who followed men through bars, red wine
spurting a sculpted arc from pouch
to mouth: tonight you sing to me
warm hands sliding down the neck of a borrowed guitar
to lie flushed as flowers at your breast, delicately
folded. I want to follow you home.

How I lost my way in Hampstead
(took a taxi home)

There is red, everywhere:
inside your mouth
each polished tabletop
plush covers on these seats
tanned men
leant over baize

outside
London rolled back, new land billows up
grey tarp with wind beneath:
we step on it and laugh, unbalancing
dry leaves, the first skeletal bushes.
we've drunk enough, our mouths
the bar grown empty now
brick buildings all around

I have no plan
you're the one
with heath-grass in your hair, red cherry on your tongue
guide me—

and then a man walks out, dark glasses
frightened dog. oh hush, you say
we must move on, he must be waiting
waiting for the dusk, someone—

your fingers sculpt the air
fumble the lit end
of a match, red cigarette, then kiss
are we now lost?
river of traffic hums below the heath
beneath all words your lips a constant smoky design

your shoulders'
pale framework caught
inside the shutters of my eye

Airport

The snow like bandages
around the windscreen
flapping open as we drive,
the car in front
tyres pressed into unrolling gauze,
our raw faces
burnt by the cold expanse of sky.
this is your terminal.
we touch, and we unpeel.
the curve of your back
branded into my arms,
dense weave of our fingers
ripping open

then we stand apart.
your face turning from me,
pink scar that heals
until it leaves no trace.

Pale winter moon come round again

Saying good-bye to you
even on street corners
is difficult

sidewalk
where we first kissed
before the cinema

strikes resonance
on every passing heel

this warmth we make
chest held to chest

wool coats
whose buttons met
then tangled accidentally

tonight our fingers mesh

your gentle face
lit by the months between
cupped in my shadowed hand

over, under

oh bright earth
dipped in darkness
how you frighten me

for Wayne

Oh sepia moon

Your downcast face
lies flat upon the water,
shivering.

this long night
feels empty as a dining room
without guests,

who will remember it?

your old-fashioned light
rattles across the surface of things,
this calm lake a tabletop
rocking with scattered pearls.

you have laid out the trees on shore
like goblets,
how their shadows trail——

even your radiance
falls second-hand.

you are nervous,
trembling.
where is the sun?

After the whale

We hold hands.
outside this rubber boat
is a new world, openness.
we watch for changes
in dark waves, patterns of light
and yet the sea won't constellate.

we have no telescope,
no shrill song of sonar
plumbing the strangeness of it all,
only ourselves, childlike,
who cannot span this mammal end to end.

crabbed fin that broke water,
small piece of moon
that grew, then turned and waned,
dark breathing hole open,
she dived, eluding us.

the water settles,
dark as night sky after a comet.
an eagle hauls its wings up on the wind.
we look to our hands, the waves

grown empty now, restless
we start the engine up,
carry this rippled stillness in.

The craft we journey in

This flickering light
our flood,
this low bed the craft
we journey in,
all streets outside
the map
we discard

for the strange peaks
of Ararat,
one white dove
spiralling

as we drift on the streams that rise

No map

We open up our hands
as pink anemones beneath water

this wide expanse of sea
between us, a slight breathing.

what is it we wait for?

our tongues emerge, muscular
as shellfish, reach deep

into the wet sand of each other's mouths.

no map tonight,

no colours joined along edges, round globe
laid flat, skull without curvature.

a new-found grid of movement
leads me to you from across the sheet,

the way your bones connect, for they at least
are making sense, my tongue now walking

up the street of your long arm,
into a city burning, full of sound and light.

Pacific rim, new year's eve

scuds of foam blown across the beach in formation, buff-coloured jellies in the wind, dark water cleans itself on rocks their blue shine spits high on impact, further out white wheels churn upon pure light the sun gilds each upturned face this satin glare suggests god's hand but not because the birds have crooked wings.

no shaft, only diffuse polishing beams. we are standing without lens or telescope above beached logs rich bloodied chipped sculpted into gloss furniture. will you remain beautiful once your hands hit mud, once your bones separate pare down into gongs or drumsticks, sundry instruments through which the light will have no grades?

i cannot catch for you the same sea, frame for you the water's leaves melted into glass, flowers of foam ripening to fruit as the sun dissolves them. the same sea as yesterday you captured in an odd slit of rock. forgive me, the salt has dimmed my sight.

Pictures of readers' wives

After the air-brushed fannies,
a family snap. Bra straps
cut into each shoulder
like reins. He won
a fiver for the shot;
she got a lifetime of remarks.

Her hands cropped,
the photograph mounted.
She likes to get it from behind.

Close up, her grainy face separates
into a map of unconnected nodes:

his off-colour jokes,
his pictures of their female dog
giving birth to puppies
wet flesh open as a centrefold,
his favourite anatomical doll—

how he takes it apart,
eyeball by rattled eyeball,
stares at the sum of parts:
nervous system, circulatory
system, lymphatic system,
transparent coil of intestines;

her beautiful, unread bones.

THE HOLLOW PLANET

Take-off: the pap smear poem

Take everything off, everything
she says, and I do,

my open legs
the point at which we meet,
her speculum
round ship
descending
into the hollow planet of my uterus.

she sees my other face,
lips of flesh
furled round a shining bud,
dark eye of nucleus
from which cells form
like petals
on the clear glass slide.

she notices/she notices not
this place I have become,
known landmarks on her map—

vagina, cervix, uterus,
the birth canal,
spine pressed in paper,
feet raised up
on metal plates—

this open-backed gown
I change into,

the fear that I may
never take it off.

Two poems for Amelia Earhart

Amelia, your broken
plane, stilled into non-sense
falls unpropelled.

I'm drawn to you.
headed for secure mainland
a dial moves, the hum in my hands changes:
it's the drag of wings through air,
strange pull
of another life.

loose waves
ungrid the earth, push back
the land's limitations—

nose turns,

wings tilt, fingers
cannot resist the steep descent
toward islands. Amelia

off course, my desire for you falls
arrow-like, cleaving the still blue air,
alters like your last flight the simple curve of the world.

II. AVIATRIX

Each ray of sun, soft rubyred canoe
I slip right through
the shadow of my feathers never held

I am flying,
towards an eggshell moon
too fragile to refuse
elbows framing the sense of it

dark inlets, let me in

breath of imagined sisters holds me up
their earth a heaven pinned down flat

this arc the one stone
I can hold, sweet kernel
of my palm
so woman-shaped, handy

melting between known worlds

this air, a mirror over which I write
A - M - E - L - I - A, defined by light

For Emily Dickinson

The sun a madwoman
spinning bright webs
around your parlour door,
the words like dust
that fell from the ceiling
and grew stems,
took root in your calico lap.
You fed them like birds
or lice
from the palm of your hand,
only opened the blinds halfway
in case the sun snatched them.
And your father,
with his suitcase of nouns
for the stern face of heaven,
asking for dinner
and pulling you
a fine thread
through the needle's eye
until you were almost
weightless,
with just your thin feet
at the doorway's path,
and death
in his strange mask
chasing you.

For Gioconda Belli

These thin fingers
have learned to close
around a gun,
and when they open,
hold a soft cup of light.
Just now, blood rises in them,
blue veins surface in the heat.

These are your hands.
They fold around your rifle,
loaded and still warm,
your hungry daughter's mouth
open beside you in a soft 'o',

the rough red linen-bound
book of your poems.
They break open
like a dam in summer,
pour words like rain
into the people's faces,
describe a season

when your black hair
fell like water
between brown banks.

Your dreams
now starve for lack of paper,
the colours of your walls
fade for lack of paint.
Words stick in your throat
and start to die there.
Your hands, light as leaves,
grow busy with a turning wind.

How do you hold a daughter
with your arms full of gun?
How will you write
if they take away your hands?

The eye of the city
is already shot blind with bombs.
All these roads crawl in circles,
choke on dust and gas.

A woman who waits
for a day-late bus
is holding your book.
Your words are her vision.
Your greatest poem lies
in the strength of her shoulders,
her refusal to walk away.

These barnacle dead

How they grip us through thin and thick,
these barnacle dead!

SYLVIA PLATH

I imagined sunlight
in Heptonstall New Cemetery,
fragments of mourning, half-buried,
your death still clear
among chrysanthemums.

But there are no guts in a graveyard.
You lie unfinished
in your busy grave, while jagged plates
in the fragile skull of earth
are silently shifting.

Each death you drew
around you was a birthday;
your name a cracked stone grown luminous with moss.

As I open the iron gate
its metal chills me.
The birds have long since emptied
their berries of seeds.
Caught in its
frozen opening
I wonder

if you sleep, what's missing now?

Mother, for a day

I spend hours
watching the sea
smash against a concrete post
breaking itself,
scattering birds.

the stormy sea—
glass trellis
shattered by a motionless fist,
tumbling
from upright sense
into the littoral,

unrolling waves
dragged back
into their own salt mouths,
incomprehensible.

la mère/la marée,
her beauty never did stand still.
a small bird, sleek with rain,
I would ride on her great salt back
for years while she hurled me
at the wall of her concrete world
and shattered me, trying
to be let in.

Mother

Tonight you phoned,
your voice uncoiled
from quiet spools of tape:
you want to fly, visit.

in this still room
its scent of discarded shoes
I touch my belly,
feel your lips
pressed against my mouth

and breathless,
turn the hall light on.

once again
I'm hauling myself
out from between your legs.

your furled womb
has never been my parachute,
its strings
have only caught round my neck.

caught up against the final beep
your stopped voice
bleeds into silence.

metal wingtips hover overhead,
red unblinking light
on my stilled answering machine,
plane that will never land.

S O

i want the baby
i couldn't have,

& the baby
i couldn't be,

to sing to me,
like angels

DI BRANDT,
mother, not mother

Corona

The moon
is a white fruit,
distant and indistinct.
My fingers
push the damp air
she is sealed in,
spread ripples
through the thickness
of a startling night,
while the unsaid
breeds beneath my tongue.

Silence coats me,
amniotic, unbirthed.

Words,
their curved universe
full of unnamed planets:

my head with its shiftless comets,
this breath full of unseen stars.

To conceive of it

Oh mummy

in the hollow of the night
while you looked through the glazed face of death
at another for the stillest motion
how i lifted you up to the half-open mouth
showed you comfort
in a breath beginning
curved between ribs and belly
like a breaking wave

then you welcomed me
deep into your atmosphere of blood
round cherry stone
bedded in an earth all my own
how i wished that your fist
would never open, bone-fist
open to the light

but the tearing pulled me
furled like a fresh wet wing
into the bare and cold

now we meet at the brink of your skin
lips on nipple, fingers clenched upon breast
we are so divided

The second heart

Curl up your fingers
in the dark, little one,
the light is out
no one is watching.
I can feel you
deep in my unclenched heart,
spiral breath
winds up your sorrow
like a cloth
wrung deep from a well.
On your rage I suck
of your grief I drink
till you grow strong enough
to be born.
Soft ear
placed upon my belly from the inside,
lips that unfold
into promises,
a way through.

Let me stay

Don't make me go: these words i sang to you nightly followed
your shuddering slowed-down guessed-at dreams from the inside
bruised gown of flesh closed loop of breath between mouth and
mouth we were not one but two centrepoint around which you
turned and fell you were outside i was inside when he hit you
opened you towards nothingness a bed a table wouldn't let you
sleep wouldn't let me sleep I'm afraid to burst afraid to leave
know that something out there is not you (all this i hear through
water without ears) you're so so trembling legs clenched around
my skull suspended i am so so harrowing whited with vernix
stalled at this slippery approach up which i must rise

for my mother

THE ENORMOUS EXIT

Confession to Frida

It was a metal rod that silenced you
then gave you voice, graphic and physical;

it was my father's body silenced me,
sinking through bone and skin,
all that I know of him is buried there.

Fragments surface:
his weight upon my chest,
long penis pulled away
from lips that weep
silent, stretched
to an impossibly wide 'O'.

I circle around this wreck,
site of my injury,
conceal its phallic shape.

My body revolves
around its single axis:
power; powerlessness.

A spine closed around its broken cord,
I still limp to accommodate
the metal rod
round which my living skin once healed,
reluctantly, shut.

When my lips break open their stitches
words lift, unpeel
the taut white face of years
that died between,

my wound
bleeds breath

that only fingers, soft consonants
can staunch
into a new scarred language,
pictures that weep.

The enormous exit

it was an enormous exit I went through, my love

FRIDA KAHLO'S JOURNAL, 1953

Four corners of solid wood:
you enter the unexpectedness of death
like entering a framed painting.

What's left
of your fierce stillness now?

Your body
sat up suddenly,
black hair fanned out,
when you entered
the furnace flame,

network of your friends' hands
frisking for jewels
sent taut with shock.

Your corpse
a fine sculpture;

each detail of your face
laid out on canvas for one finished moment

until the breeze took it,

burnt bone and ash that held your shape.

Wetness

is what you miss the most. Your womb punctured, the baby taken out, he was in small pieces. Alone with cracked dry lips, rough touch of adult skin, there is no comfort left. A wind blows among the flat pages of a medical book, ripples imagined waters that might break. You reach for your husband, but he slips away. No child, his eyes clear globes filled with unchanging light, he looks past you. You must begin again: no one has cut the cord that holds you to yourself. Pick up a brush. Inside this mother's dress a body begins to paint itself, remembers how blood sinks into white sheets, how colours saturate. This paint is sticky to the touch. Mend the rip in canvas, gather all the scattered pieces in. Still you cannot leave wetness behind. See what the doctor gave, a cold glass bottle that contains a male foetus. You want to open it, to pour such wholeness out.

Your body, the accident

A warm clay jar broken across blue tiles.
Who stoops to pick it up
why death, of course,
her fingers are spread wide:
pale veins across your nursemaid's breast
white web of rivers through dry Mexico.

Frida as man, Frida as woman

Look at my white dress
drying on the line
its lacy skirt
flutters like an angel of death
in this warm wind

it's a portrait of me
so bright and flat
none of my flesh in it:

Mother
who tucks your chubby limbs
around her own

Lover
firing small dart hands
through your big heart

Wife
who makes up lunch
in linen-lined baskets
to bring to you.

What if I cut off all my hair?
clipped off its spidery black limbs
and watched them curl
dancing, around my wooden chair

What if I wore denim, leather?
combed out my moustache
and my eyebrows, joined at the centre
like outstretched crows' wings

and flew to you,

would my white dress stand guard for us?

What is the border here?

Disintegration

Yo soy la desintegracion

TITLE OF SKETCH, 1953

My lovers are my hands,
reach in with delicate brush
to mix the colours of my frail body,

engorged flesh
that shudders
but will not break
spills out sentences,
showers the earth with my heat.

I spend my life dying.

Her searching tongue, his open fist
dissolved into my mouth,
each new finger
a violent erosion

each sudden fall
into the unmet dark,
another skin, hardening.

Death dances

Gauze next to skin
itches. White
external skeleton
tightens its grip,

the skin beneath
wrinkled as pink candy.
You must hold still.

From your bedpost
a sugar death's head
swings
in a subtle wind.

Lost picture

I find
I will return to you,
young girl
who steps knowingly
towards her own loved face.

On the long road out
to the accident,
you hold a grand piñata,
its paper belly rattling
with unseen treats.

Your stride effortless,

I want the frame
to hold you
like a ripe fruit
whose skin refuses to break.

Your smile
deflects my camera,
loosens the grip
of what's known.

Your path
become my path
become your path

untangling
towards impact.

I dream

We meet, not merely introduced, you reach, touch me, and there
is lots of red. I find I cannot breathe, fall backwards from a
lighted window, then a woman catches me. I'm taken to a party
next and you are there. We kiss. Our eyes are dark as caviar, our
breasts' rich moons dance by themselves. I cannot see your legs,
monkeys or drinking friends, only the web of your fine veins
reaching out to me. You sing: 'small daughter in a mother's skirts,
small mother in a daughter's skirts, Frida inside Frida with
nowhere else to look, no death, no life, no simple flowering
plants, one single touch that cannot be preserved . . .' Your eyes
pull me so deep I cannot hold words back but spill into waking.

This self I photograph

Your father, the photographer
whose eyes throw back the light,
behind him you paint large microbes
as if to let us in beneath his skin.
How can this represent distance?

Pictures he took of you,
sad child scarred by illness,
limbs hidden by thick olive trees,
come to represent closeness.

My father's photograph of me,
my body turned from him
as if the space between cancels
the way his fingers reached between my legs:

and how I peel from this,
as if it were a flat surface.

II.

The photographer remains unseen,
his big hands
careful to leave no mark.

In the memory
my half-developed breasts
are coming to beneath water.
Light sensitive,
I surface uncontrollably
towards his grip.

Listen to
the gentle swish
of liquid in the trays,
how I am writing him

whose careful hands
flicked the red bulb off:

I trace my pierced body
on his retina.

III.

This self I photograph:

each detail pulls from her
like unshed skin,

levels a loathsome curve
into paper.

Round girl I was,
whole woman I will become,

flat dolls
that danced me
through the middle ground

fallen into thin dark lines.

The three dimensions
of his flesh in mine
negate the possibility
of distance.

Remembrance

Death cleaves to you
she is the bald pale one holding the knife
all bone and skin turned inside out
she reconstructs you like a retablo, votive of thanks
repainted foot placed next to leg
she knows she'll get you
in the end

she holds a mask up to your face
its colours hardening
asks you to dance
she'll never leave you
in the end

her fingers stick
eye sockets widening
you turn over

she wants to send your blood
back to the earth

Memory box

Digging through sodden clay, the dirt-
dead roots that bind
me to this poisoned place
sloughed-off skins
of worm and bird

I hear cold metal clink against
my nail, raw finger
prising the hinge
clean off, to scrape a sudden sigh

from the lips
of a buried
child.

Unboxed

I find her
in the long grass,
on the low stone wall
by the house
whose worn carpeting
and blood-stained walls
she slammed the yellow door on
to leave. She packs
a dented tin with candles,
chocolate, safety pins, matches
and loose string,

calls it survival.
She wants to bury it
where no adults go.
In the crack
by the house
where I'm waiting, heavy
with old secrets, emptied
but for this
strange gift.

* * *

he comes to me at night
and touches me, separates
my legs just like the wolf does,
and the creatures
from under the bed;

I only think this
with the door closed,
through patches of bruised skin,
my undergarments
shed like orphans.

I feel the seam
along which grow-up games begin,

each night my solemn dark
is split
by one red shaft.

my doll knocked to the floor,
in bleeding innocence

I hear my baby
crying, and I
lock her up, rip
her nice new dress,
and make her grow up

secretly
in a hidden place
where no one plays,
and little girls choke
on the dirt of daddy

Without hope

TITLE OF PAINTING, 1945

When I pull back the drapes
of my dress each night
when I let down my hair
all I hear is the clanking of shears—
all that has been, all that is
to be taken from me.

When I slice my flesh open
and divide in two
there's a part that remains
unexhibited:

it's my own wounding

worlds you cannot see

beneath my face and shirts
a broken-roofed temple
held up by metal pins

all pistons, wheels
that turn and work, unseen

unspoken words
piled up in my mouth
eggs that turn inside my ovaries
unused

this anger
held back in my fingers' ends:

onlooker, put away your shears
you cannot take this loss away from me.

Stand separate

Your body is not mine
no more than England's
loneliest white coast
can signal home.

My own body,
toxic familiarity,
each poem a loose road
that turns, switches
and leads me to
another strange landfall.

No bright star leads me on.

You have no substance left
yet I trawl you for treasures
that were lost, yet I use you
to decorate
the dull prow of my pain.

You are no carved angel.

Even the dust has changed,
the language in Mexico.

Smoke pours from the grates
in my home town,
articulates lost words for hidden fire.
What signal reaches you?

The face you left
smiles slightly, unchanging.

I turn my ships around.

I write

Your paint
is your blood, smeared
onto brown skin of canvas
dried and cracked into a scar
clear as the shape of Mexico.

Here grows a new texture,
a page between wound and world.

I draw your hand
moving like a tram
along its chosen rails,
to slip and stab the canvas
in a place that cuts your body free
from the burning wreck.

You are the aggressor now.
On the outside of your skin
pain stays in its place,
stilled at the moment of collision.

Each line I write separates two fields.
This I know, this I don't know.
This I am, this I am not.

I borrow your mask and brush,
print your colours over everything I touch;
I have not worn your hands.

The words between us tilt
into a sloping shore, fade
like the blue smoke of mountains.

I am the aggressor here,
I write upon the outside of my skin
the names of England,
the rip in my heart that is home
and the truth that dries in there,
hardened to a pip.

A few small nips

TITLE OF PAINTING, 1935

Spiked through by metal rods,
greased hands of some doctor,
you lie opened.

Curve of your pelvic bone
a watershed.

Light moves on it,
all angry distances.
You did not ask for this.

On leaving England

I have hiked across the hills' rough spine
to the highest ground, treeless, farmed-out,
pitted with worked-out mines,
rugged with grit and moss;
I have pulled myself to an edge of calm
above the roads' abyss,
broad ridge that crests
above the hazy plain

to feel the softness of a land in me
that accepts rain and thunder,
great limestone/millstone shell
that gives and resists, gives and resists
until there is nothing left.

You'll find no decoration here,
no flowers or trees,
only my bare white legs
flapping against torn cloth,
a square of earth that cradles me
like a blunt and calloused hand.

You'll find no explanation here
for my father's bitterness,
my mother's emptiness,
for I have turned my grief
into the silent face of the fells,
I have turned my suffering
into a drystone wall.

I'm all alone
with the rock of my bones
that will follow me
across the ocean floor
to Canada.

Shielded by the sky's white helmet,
I beat the sullen grass with my fists,
scream at the mucky rock
for truthfulness, this sudden watershed,
the trickle that forms, peaty and black
between cobs of moss
then courses, pitiful,
down to an unknown sea.

The two Fridas

TITLE OF PAINTING, 1939

Side by side, we do not touch
the self I've lived
the self I barely know
split at the moment of impact.
Two stretched lips
of a single wound
one bleeds, the other's dry.

You weep everywhere,
in books, on cards, on calendars,
your crying heals me:
between the silent painted bells
of the calla lily
your outstretched arms uncover roses,
their delicate curves
are not part of the backdrop
but sculptures of women inventing love.

Floating against a blue storm
I fill up arteries of sound,
caught in the vice between continents
I am the hard-won space
that articulates paired bones.

Our masks have fallen from their plaster stem.
Cold fingers creep together through the void,
one strong fist that protects a subtle union
with the power of two closed hands.

Transparency

Sentences
that close round pigment
truer than I have ever seen

fingers of breath
untangling the body's line

each incandescent sheet
held out to frame

the just heat
that lingers
after long silence

They ask for planes
(and only get straw wings)

TITLE OF PAINTING, 1938

The way he entered me
between deaf walls
his hard flesh carved
into my soft surfaces

weight pressed to my throat
the great tongue choking me

half-whispered threats
wet mouth that never matched
the words he spoke
length of his tongue
red at breakfast:

now with my adult limbs
I can unlearn
the language of his white body

I will uncover him

the skin that separates
his flesh from mine
bare hands will pull me through

hot silence branded into me

my voice articulates

each tight lip
slowly opens:

his body after death
still as an unlit match
safe in its box, no flame burning

my body laid out on the bed
my spirit burnt, raging.

    for my father

Viva la vida

Your single leg hidden beneath blankets, you decorate your final plaster cast with iodine, small mirrors, photographs of absent friends. You paint insides of things, turn them around: dull skin of melon cracked open to reveal red lips that wait for your tongue, slim frantic brush or finger to make love to. You find each place where green rind breaks and wetness spills out, possibility: the path of each blind pip that rolls towards sunlight. Your square canvas has become a field, a place of sand or snow in which your fingers hope to sculpt

the way you touch, the way you speak a name, how you once danced as if pain didn't bother you, your wooden leg that never gives in to the touch. The place your right foot was pulses and agitates you still.

Stilled life

Frida, come dance around this flame
your only spine, white-hot pivot
from which limbs hang

you'll find a ribbon rippling
through your black hair

colours that come
tripping like anxious friends

you'll tease them out
with your bright lips
shy animals, magenta red
this flesh in which you live
its bare mountains

and when the heat flares up
burns all your colours into none
there will be pieces left

corsets, legends
the curtain round your bed
in the blue house
jingling with shattered light

About the Author

ALEXA BERTON

CATHY STONEHOUSE was born and grew up in the northwest of England. She has a B.A. in English from Wadham College, Oxford University and in 1988 was awarded a Commonwealth Scholarship to study Creative Writing at the University of British Columbia, receiving her Master of Fine Arts in 1990. Her poems have been published in a variety of journals in Canada and England. She lives in Vancouver with her partner and two cats, and is working on a novel and a second book of poems.

About the Artist

IAN STONEHOUSE lives in a small house somewhere in England with a cat and a lot of trees. He makes music, pictures and films. He can't drive, isn't married and doesn't mind.

PRESS GANG PUBLISHERS FEMINIST CO-OPERATIVE is committed to producing quality books with social and literary merit. We give priority to Canadian women's work and include writing by lesbians and by women from diverse cultural and class backgrounds. Our list features vital and provocative fiction, poetry and non-fiction.

A free catalogue is available from Press Gang Publishers, 101-225 East 17TH Avenue, Vancouver, B.C., Canada V5V 1A6